Endless Possibilities

by the Eighth Grade Students of
Mt. Juliet Middle School
Mt. Juliet, Tennessee

Mrs
Baragu
thanks
4 always
been
there
for
me
since
Kinder
garden

Landa
(ElEm)

WRITE TOGETHER PUBLISHING
Nashville, Tennessee

Published by Write Together Publishing ™ LLC.
www.writetogether.com

ISBN   1-931718-26-1 Paperback

Title: Endless Possibilities.
Author: Various.
Subject: Literary collections, poetry.

Project Coordinator: Anne Barger
Cover Art: Ronisha Fletcher

For Write Together Publishing:

Publisher: Paul Clere

Editor-in-Chief: John D. Bauman

Art Director: Bill Perkins

Publishing Representative: Michael Pleasant

To publish a book for your school or non-profit organization that complements
your academic goals or values, vision and mission, please contact:

Write Together ™ Publishing
533 Inwood Dr.
Nashville, TN 37211

phone: 615-781-1518
fax: 520-223-4850
www.writetogether.com

Chelsea Martin

Ronisha
Jones
you
did HaHa

lynsie
McElroy

Dre—
Rogers

Table of Contents

I Wish 49

Night 57

Menagerie 77

Mt. Juliet Middle School
1003 Woodridge Place
Mt. Juliet, TN 37122
615-754-6688
Fax 615-754-7566

Mike Gwaltney
Principal

Anne Barger
Asst. Principal

Dear Reader,

We celebrate the insight and thoughts our students have shared in the pages of *Endless Possibilities*. The middle school years are years of incredible change for young people, years in which their views of the world and life are affected by their experiences.

We applaud our students' writing, and we invite you to learn more about the middle school student through the thoughts they have shared in this book.

Enjoy!

Mike Gwaltney
Principal
Mt. Juliet Middle School

Endless Possibilities

My life holds endless possibilities that
I know I can make come true.
I am going to strive for the dreams
I know I can do.

Allison Pulley

There are unlimited numbers of possibilities, whether one minute or one year in the future. It seems as though life goes by fast. There's no way we can make it stop, but there is a reason for its passing. People are always concentrating and basing their lives on things they don't have that they want, instead of on being grateful and enjoying the things they do have. Just being alive is something special. Of course, we don't think that most of the time, but it is.

Change is something to which we have many varied reactions. We're either sad or excited about change, or our feelings may be in-between. We don't know what's to come in the future. Possibilities are endless in our lives and endless in our world. The chance to change in the future is not up to anyone else but us.

Something important to do right now is making goals in your life. Goals are crucial to your future, even if they're small. If you have goals set that you want to achieve, then that's wonderful. With goals, your life keeps going on. You have a reason to get up every morning. Your life has meaning. You strive to achieve your goals every day. That's going to end up helping you in the future.

You have to work for everything that you get; nobody is going to hand you a card that says, "You're the richest person in the world." You pick your possibilities. You're choosing right now who you want to be and become; that's how it works. Your dream future profession changes as you change; so, as you grow older, try to go by your strengths and weaknesses.

Possibilities are great for anything. Possibilities can be horrible and magnificent; the world comes with both. We don't notice it, but the future is already happening.

Diadora Lago

As I walk into my middle school
I dream, I hope, I pray
That my teachers will mold me
Into what I may become someday.

It's amazing how far I've come
In my thirteen years of age,
But I've still got my whole life to live
And things to accomplish along the way.

My life holds endless possibilities that
I know I can make come true.
I am going to strive for the dreams
I know I can do.

Allison Pulley

The endless possibilities that occur throughout our world will never stop until the human race ceases to exist. Whatever you think of can come true. People have been wishing to be able to fly for thousands of years, and it finally came true in 1903.

People invented a huge ship called the *Titanic*. Who would ever think we could create a free-standing building thousands of feet tall? Well, we did. If we can think it up, we can create it. That's what the human race has proved throughout its existence so far.

Kyle Hardy

Endless possibilities.
A colorful future.
Advances in medicine and technology.
The sky is no longer the limit.
Go farther!
Inventions flourishing.
New people.
New things.
Maybe even new places.
Life on Mars could be reality
Instead of just a dream.
For the future,
The possibilities are endless.

Angel Nixon

"Endless possibilities" reminds me of the poem *The Road Not Taken* by Robert Frost. Every crossroad we come to in life has a different possibility, a different ending. The choices we make influence our lives. The choice could be a wise one; unfortunately, it could be horrible as well. Sometimes there are mixed consequences. Yet, thank goodness, there are always those endless possibilities to fall back on.

Rachel Stephens

Life has many endless possibilities. What will you do when you grow up? Whom will you marry? Will you have any children? If so, will it be a boy or a girl? Or both? Which road will you choose to go down? Will you be happy? Will you be glad you chose the career you chose?

I have no idea what the answers are to these questions for my life. Anything is possible. You could have your life all planned out, then something could happen, and all your plans could change. You may think that what you want to do is not right for you or think that you could not reach the goals you have. But if you work really hard, you can achieve your goals. Life has several different endless possibilities.

Ashley Hutton

What are endless possibilities?
Life?
Love?
School?
What does it include?
Girls?
Boys?
Animals?
Our heads are filled with many
ambitions about life,
love, and school.
We don't know what
to think about our
futures;
the possibilities are endless.
We are scared of what we
want and what we
dream.
We hope to move
on with our lives; to
separate our dreams
and hopes from reality.

Endless possibilities are ours.

Rachel Sedgwick

Out in the world there are endless possibilities. These possibilities depend on whether you want to go to college or go straight to the "real world" when you get out of high school. There are many possibilities for you; you just need to know what you would like to do.

Once you excel during your college or high school years, you probably want to seek a job. You can achieve anything if you set your mind to it. I know you have heard that before, but I truly believe this. I have achieved many things in this manner. For example, I want to play professional baseball, so right now I am playing on the junior high team, practicing at every opportunity, making good grades, and always trying to make correct moral choices. If I continue to do this, then hopefully I will have a better chance to achieve my goals in life.

In our country there are endless possibilities and opportunities in which to achieve your goals. Accompanying achievement is knowing that you have accomplished what you have set out to do.

Jerry McMurtry

The possibilities are endless
When it comes to our future.
The sky's the limit.
No one can say for sure
What we have in store for us,
And it is for the best that we
Keep it that way.

There are times in our lives
When unexpected events occur,
Events that we cannot change
Or do anything about.
So never give up your dreams.
Always strive to do the best you can
For you'll never know
What you can achieve
Until you've tried.

Kari Garrett

7

Anything is possible for you and me.
Possibilities are endless like the wide, open sea.

Our world has only endless possibilities today.
The sky's the limit is what some say.

Our dreams and wishes can come true,
If we take given possibilities and see them through.

The possibilities are all around us,
Use them to their full potential is something we must.

Possibilities will come and go,
Like the soft touch of winds blown.

Several possibilities await us in our future,
To treat them like treasures is sure.

They say opportunity only knocks once for everyone,
But there are endless knocks on the doors of possibility
that we mustn't shun.

Ashley Back

Thank you so much for everything.
Ashley Back

I believe America is the greatest country in the world. Other countries envy the great opportunities we have to offer. Without our freedom, this would not be true.

My definition of freedom in a country is to be able to speak and live freely without the government trying to run your life. Our freedom does come with a price. Thousands of men and women have fought and died for our country. Without them, we would not have the freedoms and rights we have today.

"Freedom's not bought with dust," is a famous quote from Harriet Tubman. Her particular struggle for freedom is no longer an issue in the U.S., but her words can refer to all kinds of freedom. America's freedom was not bought with any one thing. It was achieved by the sacrifice of human life. If we want it badly enough, America has endless possibilities.

Jonathan Robbins

I Used to Be

I used to be a baby
Small and sweet
But now I'm a teenager
Independent and changing every minute

Paige McFarlin

ENDLESS POSSIBILITIES

I used to be a seed
    Small and unchanging
But now I am a garden
    Beautiful
    Growing and changing every day

I used to be a caterpillar
    Slow, fat and ugly
But now I am a butterfly
    Beautiful and graceful

I used to be a kitten
    Puny and helpless
But now I am a cat
    Strong, clever, and cunning

Molly Reed

I used to be a baby
Small and sweet
But now I'm a teenager
Independent and changing every minute

I used to be a caterpillar
Slow and wandering around the world
But now I'm a butterfly
Flying through life discovering and learning

I used to be a kitten
With big curious eyes
But now I'm a cat
Sly as can be

Paige McFarlin

I used to be a cat
Calm, shy and kept to myself
But now I am a tiger
Proud, king, and dominant

I used to be a sun
Shinning bright and strong
But now I am just a black hole
Sitting alone in space

I used to be a bubble
Floating high in the sky
But now I am popped
Dead on the ground

Stacy Crawford

I used to be a baby
Curious and kind but now I'm older
Still curious
But also knowing a lot more

I used to be a puppy
Playful and strong
But now I'm an old dog
Lazy and weak

I used to be a tiny plant
Filled with nutrients and growth
But now I'm a huge tree
Dry and dead

Jodi Smith

I used to be a caterpillar
Crawling through the night
But now I am a butterfly
Soaring above

I used to be a child
So little and close-minded
But now I am a teenager
With strength and determination

I used to be a stump
In the ground
But now I am a majestic oak

Jerri Smith

I used to be a ship
Sailing across the sea
But now I'm a rotten piece of wood
Lying on a sandy beach

I used to be a caterpillar
Climbing on the leaves
But now I'm a pretty butterfly
Flying around the trees

I used to be a seed
Planted deep in the ground
But now I'm an apple
On someone's plate

Brandy Dickens

I used to be peaceful
With the world at my feet
But now I'm at war
With bin Laden's retreat

I used to be a caterpillar
Trapped in a cocoon
But now I'm a butterfly
With the ability to zoom

I used to be safe
But now am in danger of
Being attacked
By a stranger

Tom Cothran

I used to be a flower
Blooming in the sun
Beautiful as can be
But now winter has come
Freezing up the ground
And I lie here waiting
Waiting for the sun to come around

I used to be a ship
Dancing on the water
Without a care in the world
But now I'm a sunken ship
With treasures hidden deep within

I used to have a very good friend
Almost like an older brother
But now God has picked him out
Both still heavy on our hearts

Ashley Burrows

I used to be an egg
Confined from the world, trapped within myself
But now I am a bird
Free and soaring
Always chattering

I used to be new
Fresh and nothing wrong with me
But now I am worn
With a few scratches and bumps

I used to be a tree
Full of life and peace
But now I am lumber
Ready to be made into something
That will last

I used to be a sparrow
Not sure what I was going to do
But now I am an eagle
Soaring after my dreams

I used to be
A new computer
With a fresh memory
But now I am
A full hard drive
Adding on extra space for more knowledge

I used to be a mouse
Small and defenseless
But now I am
An ever-growing bear
Scaring off anyone who comes near

I used to be a lake
Live and watery as can be
But now I am a desert
Barren and dry

ENDLESS POSSIBILITIES

I used to be a tadpole
Swimming freely on my own
But now I am a frog
Jumping and hopping
All day long

I used to be a caterpillar
Fuzzy and green
But now I am an elegant butterfly
Bright and colorful

Woody Hatchett

I used to be a raindrop
All alone
But now I'm a puddle
With many friends

I used to be a tadpole
Small and tiny
But now I'm a frog
Big and warty

I used to be a liquid
Boiling hot
But now I'm a solid
Freezing cold

Stacey Leaver

I used to be a bald head,
With all worries sliding off me
But now I have a full head of hair
Snagging all worries and problems

I used to be a chapter in a book
With not much to say
But now I'm a novel
With lots of words to say

I used to be a caterpillar
Getting picked on by birds
But now I'm a butterfly
With bright wings to fly from birds

Steven Dukic

I used to be
A fire,
Burning really bright
I was a huge flame
I lit up the night
But now I'm ash
I thought I would last
I thought wrong
That time has passed

I used to be a seed,
I started really small
Back then I was a runt
I had to take the fall
But now I am a tree
I'm really filled with pride
Now that I am so big
You can't see the other side

I used to be a tree
Yes that was me
They cut me down
I had a frown

Daniel Keaton

I used to be a bud
Just waiting to come out
But now I am a flower
Opening up to new things

I used to be a caterpillar
Inching along
But now I am a butterfly
Spreading my wings and flying

I used to be a sapling
Standing small and afraid
But now I am a tree
Standing tall and proud

Lauren Bischoff

I used to be a raindrop
Soaring through the air
But now I am a water puddle
Extending everywhere

I used to be a teenager
Thinking I could never die
But now I am a mother
Watching my baby cry

I used to be a page
Flipping from side to side
But now I am a book
Holding all of my papers inside

Cortney Edmondson

ENDLESS POSSIBILITIES

I used to be a tree
Standing mighty and tall
Up above everything
But now I'm a stump
Growing older

I used to be a gymnast
Flipping and tumbling were my thing
Strong I was
But now I am in guard
Trying to be the best
That I can be
Trying to forget all my worries
And be strong all the time

I used to be a fish
Swimming around
But now I'm still a fish
Searching for what I
Think is right

Chelsey Ruegge

I used to be a little cub
    Running and jumping around
But now I am a roaring lion
    Ready to defend what's mine

I used to be a new basketball
    Ready and willing to play
But now I am an old ball
    Tired, ragged, and all worn out

I used to be a small puppy
    Courageous and pouncing about
But now I am a large dog
    Easy going and just not caring

Robin Crowell

ENDLESS POSSIBILITIES

I used to be a kitten
Cute and fuzzy as can be
But now I am a sly cat
Ready to pounce on anything
That walks by

I used to be a sapling
Very small and fragile
But now I am a tree
Big and strong, towering over others

I used to be a bug
A nuisance to those around me
But now I'm a butterfly
So beautiful to see

Natalie Kent

Changes

As we face life's changes,
Good, bad, happy, or sad,
We should appreciate and rejoice
In the life that we've had.

Taryn Martin

As I gaze into the mirror, I see an unfamiliar person. She resembles someone that I used to know, but at the same time she is so different. A young woman now stands in the place of a child. When did this happen?

At least a couple of years have passed since I last took a really good look at myself. The once long and frizzy red hair is now chopped off and tamed, and now over my bluish-green eyes rest a pair of glasses. The previously chubby, childish look has matured into a thinner figure with a new, natural glow.

Along with the new appearance, she now bears something new and unusual. She finds herself with emotions she had never before expressed. She may cry for any reason, or even have a bad day when everything goes her way. These feelings are uncontrollable, and even she gets confused by them.

This sense of young adulthood has its share of both happiness and sadness, but the trip alone is worth the ride between being a child and an adult.

Katy Haynes

Change is inevitable.
Then there's the good things
We see it every day.
That make our spirits rise.
We see it at work,
Things other than death,
At school, and at play.
Destruction, and the incessant lies.

A family member dies.
Think of the look
We lose a best friend.
On a new father's face
Our country is attacked,
When he sees the addition
The mood changes yet again.
He made to the human race.

The things we take for granted,
As you can see,
Like the sky and the trees,
Things constantly change,
Are destroyed every day,
Whether it's expected,
Along with the air we breathe.
Probable, or strange.

Curtis Beekley

Many changes have come to me.

My view of things, my acts, my family—all are being tested to see if they can make the transition.

Not nine months ago, my family of three at the time moved from our apartment into the area of Green Hills on the boundary of Wilson County. Though it was not my choice, we chose a great house in a terrible neighborhood. For seven years, we lived with people constantly moving in and out all around us. I was doing great in school, and I was going to have a new baby sister. We were no longer going to be a family of three, but of four. Not long after my sister's birth, my father was diagnosed with cancer, a cancer that was untreatable.

An unstoppable disease left me once again part of a three-person family.

Not longer than six months passed, and we moved to a large neighborhood where we knew many of the people. However, our school was the same, and in two years I would be in junior high.

Before I reached junior high, my great grandmother moved to Mt. Juliet from her apartment in Pennsylvania. She was 93 years old and always needed constant attention. That task fell to my sister and me. Junior high came and things were calm until September 11, 2001. That day changed not only me, but the entire nation. Though not directly affecting me, I realized how much devastation can be caused within one hour, one minute or one second. I realized not to take for granted the gift of life. Instead, we should live life to the fullest, not procrastinate, and accomplish what we are meant to do on this earth.

Jay Gillispie

Everything in this world is changing,
And almost everything is always rearranging.
Some are the for the good, some are for the bad.
Some make you happy, others make you sad.
Let's start with boys and girls.
That is what makes this world.
Girls like guys; some go out,
Some are good, some have doubt.
Girls get hurt, but boys don't care.
Just remember that some will always be there.
You'll change schools and make new friends.
Just remember that's not always the end.
You'll get married and have some kids,
Then you'll probably die, but they will live.
They will carry on in your place for you.
They will be thankful for what they do, because it's for you.
Your body will change throughout your life,
And you will want to cut some people out of your life.
You will love people, and you hate them too.
No matters what happens, your friends will see you through.
People will change, and so will you.
Yet, somehow your changes will leave you the same.
You will grow stronger, mentally and physically.
In your life, you will not always be happy.
Sometimes you will be angry and sad.
But don't worry, someone or something will make you glad,
Glad you're in this world, glad you have a life,
Or, perhaps, glad that you did not change.
You might or might not.

Tina Jaramillo

We all lost something or someone on the morning of September 11, 2001. Some lost a husband or wife. Others lost parents or children. Friends and loved ones were gone in seconds. People across America lost their sense of safety and peace. Those who previously had selfishly cared only about themselves were seen helping others. No matter where you were, no matter what you were doing, you were affected by the events that occurred that Tuesday, though you may not even realize it.

Changes are taking place everywhere. They may happen in different ways, at different times, and for different people, but they happen in the life of every person. For some, it's the adjustments they have to make when they lose someone close to them. For others it may be having a loved one go to war and not knowing if they will return.

Change is everywhere. It follows us. It surrounds us. It never stops. It never hesitates. It goes on forever. Change is good, and it is evil. It is the never-ending cycle of life.

Change is sometimes difficult to deal with; but if we help each other through the tough times, all will be right again.

This is dedicated to those who lost their lives in the tragedy of September 11, 2001. Gone, but not forgotten, they will live forever in our hearts.

Ashley Daniel

There have been many changes that have taken place in my life. When I was five years old, I moved from Franklin, Tennessee, to Mt. Juliet. About a year later, my parents got a divorce.

I was so upset because my dad moved back to Franklin to live with my grandmother. I only get to see him every other weekend, but all that is going to "change." He got remarried and is looking for a house here in Mt. Juliet closer to me and my sister.

Then two years ago, my great-grandfather died. It hurt me because we were close. We always visited him and my great-grandmother after church every Sunday, and we would always eat lunch together. Then another of my family members died. It was my grandfather. We weren't all that close, but it really hurt my grandmother.

My mom just bought a new SUV. It's pretty nice. She's keeping her old car for me to drive. Then on October 31, 2001, I turned 14. I was real excited. The thing that excited me the most was the fact I would be driving in one year.

The event that changed all our lives took place on September 11, 2001. A terrorist attack struck the New York City Twin Towers, killing thousands. When we declared war, that's when all our lives were changed.

That's all the events that have taken place up till now, but I'm sure that there's more to come!

Kyle Cheek

Change controls our every move
Though this definition is very crude.
It determines our feelings and emotions.
It derives from peoples' lively notions.
Change is good, and change is bad.
It can make you frustrated and mad.
Change is for the better and change is for the worse.
Change can be at home or all around the world.
Change follows us everywhere.
You can change your clothes or the color of your hair.
Your parents might get a divorce,
And you are forced to go back and forth.
Maybe this will help you understand the word
Change.

Marquis' Wilson

As I gazed upon the TV screen, I looked in awe at what used to be one of the most recognizable landmarks in the greatest country in the world. Concrete and twisted metal buried innocent people in the rubble. It looked like a scene from a movie.

Millions of Americans knew that this horrific event would bring with it great change. America, finally united, stepped back to consider what is really important. This surge in patriotism will forever change America. The greatest part of our country, the spirit of its people, shines brightest in its darkest hour. For the first time in many years, the people of our country are proud to be Americans.

Russell Freda

Change can mean
so many things. It
can be minor or major,
good or bad. Sometimes
it can even be very sad!
Change can affect you
mentally, or it can affect
you physically. It
doesn't have to be life
threatening; it can be
just as little as changing
your schedule. It can
be accomplishing
something important
or something small.
Most of the time, it
comes when you least
expect it! You can like
it or hate it, but either
way, you always have
to face it!

Dawn Decker

My life has changed so much since God entered into my heart. I know that I wouldn't be the same person I am today without His help. I know that I wouldn't be a good person or a good friend if I didn't have the guidance of God.

One thing that God has blessed me with in my life is the relationships I have with my three best friends. I met them through church and school. My personal relationships with them have brought me closer to God, and I have brought them closer to Him, also.

Not only did God give me my three best friends, but He gave me my ability to play softball along with two wonderful coaches whom I love to death. Another gift He has blessed me with is the gift of listening.

I am a great friend to everyone, or at least I try to be. Most of my friends always come to me in their times of need, and I am grateful for that.

I am so thankful for God and the many blessings He's given me. He's changed my life in so many ways, shapes, and forms.

Bailey Crick

You are faced with change
    As you begin each day.
You have to face them and
    Not run away.

Changes can be seen
    All around,
From the time the sun comes up
    Until it goes down.

People change from
    Young to old,
Life is precious and
    Worth more than gold.

As we face life's changes,
    Good, bad, happy, or sad,
We should appreciate and rejoice
    In the life that we've had.

Taryn Martin

Change is a very important thing in life. There are changes in your environment and changes physically. Take, for example, the tragedy in New York City. When I first heard the news, I was really shocked. The victims' families must have had a great deal of change in their lives.

Although the tragedy didn't happen here, and I didn't have any family members hurt or missing, it changed me a great deal. I know some people whose lives are changed by this, and I am trying to help them. I went to New York over the summer and saw the Twin Towers. But now I know that was my last chance to see them since they have now collapsed.

Sometimes change can be good, and it can also be bad. I am moving next year to Old Hickory, and that means this is my last school year here. But this could also be good because we'll get a new house, and I will meet some new friends. Although I won't see my old friends as often, I can phone them or e-mail them. Since I will have a new house, new friends, and go to a new school, it will be like starting a new life.

Even though you don't always like change, it has to happen. Change can't always be a bad thing, but it can't always be a good thing either.

I have also changed by having more knowledge. When I was younger, I didn't know all that I know now. I have learned more and more in each grade.

In conclusion, change is everywhere and anywhere, whether it's good or bad.

Ada Leung

Changes come
And changes go.
Decisions will be tossed
To and fro.
Out of a deck
Pull one card.
The card you choose
Is all you have.
But other choices
Will come around,
So wait and be patient
Because good times will come.
And when that day comes
    Have fun!

This is your only life
So treat it nicely.
Changes will come
And they may be pricey.
Some things happen
That change your life
For example,
    A wife!

When a change comes
That you dislike
Just remember one thing:
    That's life!

As a tulip blooms in the spring
And as it sways with the breeze,
It is here for a short time.
And when fall comes,
It goes away.
That is a change
And it happens every day.
Seasons come.
Rain hums.
Changes are wonderful
    To everyone!

Taylor Cheney

Colors

Aqua the feeing when you
Dip your toes in the warm seawater

Aqua the feeling of when
The minnows are swimming hurriedly
Past your legs

Elizabeth Harned

Vermillion

Vermillion reminds me of my broken love
Identified as the roaring volcano of anger I feel
Vermillion the color of the ball of hidden fears
Buried deep inside me
But alas the color of a pretty rose
A new love has arisen

Jessica Young

Black

Black, the color of the midnight sky
Being so dark there in its place
Black is the color of mystery
Also the color of misery
Black is the color of loneliness
Sitting there alone drowning by yourself
Black by itself

Donnie Gray

Silver

A pretty girl is a girl with glittering
Shiny pearls, the way her eyes glare.

Silver is the color of lots of money
That glistens like a whole bunch
Of yummy honey,
It's not the color of a pretty bunny.

Silver shines in pretty clouds, shining
Over people's sounds,
Silver is the lucky coin on the campground.

Ryan Self

Green

Green is the color
Of trees
Green is the color
Of leaves
Green is the color
Of my eyes
Green isn't the color
Of the skies
Green brought the color
To the seas
Green things happen
Out of seeds
Green is built upon
The docks
Green is the color
Of the world from space
In which a smile should
Appear on every face

Tiffany Brewer

41

White

White
The color of a beautiful
Angel that watches over you
White
The color of pure trust
And innocence

Christian Gibson

Blue

Blue, the color of the ocean
I can smell the scent of salt in the air
I feel the wind blowing through my hair
When I think of blue

The rustle of the waves
Brings me back
To a time I almost forgot
But I remember the solitary color of my summer

Blue were his eyes
And my skirt
And his shirt
As we walked along a sea of blue

Blue, the color I will always remember
For it was the color of our love
That was sent from above
But alas it's now gone

Amanda Allison

Aqua

Aqua the feeing when you
Dip your toes in the warm seawater

Aqua the feeling when
The minnows are swimming hurriedly
Past your legs

Aqua the feeling of a cool
Sea breeze on a hot summer's day

Aqua the soothing sound of
The water rushing to the shore

Elizabeth Harned

Black

Black is the color of a closed box
That has the scent of fear
When you are lost and frightened
And no one is near
Black is the dust covering you
When you are yelling,
When all you hear is whispering
It shuts you out from everything
All you are now is part of it

Blake Russell

Yellow

Yellow is the color of the sun with bright rays of light.
It cuts through the sky.
It makes people smile at me.
Yellow, what a wonderful color.

Donnie Holder

Red

Red is the color of love,
And the color of excitement.
It is a mood
That says you're feeling good.
Like that smile
Stretching mile after mile.

Blake Giles

Green

Green is a great color,
Cool as could be.
Green is the leaf
That fell from a tree.
Green is also a color in camouflage.
Now should you really see me?

Matt Tyler

Blue

Blue is the color of cerulean skies
That children play under near and far.
Blue could also be the color of winter
And of the cold that comes
With it through the form of snow and ice.
It is the color of the sea
That runs for miles under
The cerulean skies.

Kyle Conder

Amethyst

Amethyst is the color of royalty,
Of gorgeous things,
Of beautiful rings.
Amethyst is a birthstone,
It is clear and purple,
And shines like the sun off of the sea.

Jessie Barton

Aqua

Aqua
A tropical sea
With waves of fury
A glimmering,
Luminous,
Fantasy.

Karen Smith

Green

Green is the glossy color of the ocean,
Twinkling in the sun.
Green is the velvety color of trees and plants,
The color of life itself.
Green is a cheerful color.
Soothingly, it makes you happy and glad.

David Hill

Topaz

Topaz is the sun shining through
My window that awakens me
In the morning
Topaz is the glow on my face
As I walk down the stairs and
See my family sitting at the kitchen table
As I look out the window
I see yellow roses and bumble bees
Flying all around them
That is topaz

Drew Kuchta

Blue

Blue bubbles floating all around
Blue is the color of foamy seas
Splashing over the rocks on the coast
Blue–raspberry candy
Tingling in your mouth
Blue is the color of clear skies
Bombarded with planes tearing through it
Blue eyes glisten in the light
Blue is the color of sadness and tears
Blue is just a strange feeling
That no one can explain

Catherine Runyon

I Wish

I wish
People were always in a good mood
And never down
Always smiling
And never frowning

Sydney Richardson

I wish
People were not
So demanding and
Took their time
With things

I wish
People would understand
How lucky they are to be living

I wish
I could achieve
My dreams
And be successful
At what I will
Be able to do

Amanda Smith

*Amanda
Smith*

I wish
That I could travel around
The world. From the white
Beaches in Cancun to the
Roaring snow-covered Mt. Everest

I wish
That I could visit heaven to
Greet and meet my ancestors and
Others that I have never met

I wish
That we had peace around us
Not bombing and shooting

I wish
That people would just think
Before they do something

Ashley Taylor

I wish
That people could
Be themselves around
Their friends

I wish
That people would
Not put down
Other people
Because they think
It amusing and funny

I wish
That people would
Turn around and
Say no to drugs
And alcohol

Charlie Stanfield

I wish
That the sun shone on the ground
Spreading warmth over it
And I could enjoy sitting in the shade more often

I wish
The air would always smell like it just rained
I could capture the beauty of the dew
Sparkling in the sun
And I could enjoy the mornings just as they are
Calm and peaceful

I wish
The grass would always be bright green
It would be smooth and damp
And I could watch the grass move every time
A soft wind blew

Casey Baker

I wish
People had more money
And they all would have a home
They all would have a phone

I wish
People went to church
To stay free from evil

I wish
Everyone had a family
To help them when in need
So they could be the best
They could be

Brandon King

ENDLESS POSSIBILITIES

I wish
People did not judge
They need to meet you
Before they decide who you are

I wish
That everyone was more appreciating
Of the world we live in
And the people that live in it

I wish
People were always in a good mood
And never down
Always smiling
And never frowning

Sydney Richardson

I wish
We had a winning season
We would have won just one game
We weren't 0-8

I wish
We won a game
Our team would play right
We didn't lose

I wish
Our offense would have blocked
Our defense would have tackled
We had won

Josh Eurton

ENDLESS POSSIBILITIES

I wish
I could explore more beyond
To meet new people and make new friends
To go beyond limits and expectations
To explore the unknown

I wish
To understand why parents put teens
Through torture and pain
To be understood by what I might do
To be unmistaken by others who hear me

I wish
Not to be judged by my outside appearance
To be treated like anyone else that
Thinks they are higher in class
For everyone to understand that no
One is more special than
The other

Annie Boswell

ENDLESS POSSIBILITIES

I wish
That I could take
The wishbone off of a
Turkey and get the
Bigger piece so my
Wishes would come true

I wish
My brain worked like
A computer, but instead all it
Does is download

I wish
School had a pool
So I could go swimming when
I get bored, that would be cool

I wish
We could be like pictures
So we would never get old

Adam Sullivan

Night

The gloaming dim of the eve invades all five senses. Hear the rustling of the leaves, breathe the bitterness of the air and smell the moisture and dewy grass.

Rebecca Wilkinson
Kathleen Willoughby

The expanse of the heavens entered the atmosphere as the darkness shadowed the night sky. Calmly, the death of the day emerged to life. As the night fell, people drifted away and the nocturnal sounds arose.

The night fell and the last meal was to come. The sky froze with darkness covering all.

Calmly and peacefully, black velvet silhouetted the city, as the light began to rise and reign again.

Jenni Bodine
Lisa Palmer

The falling shadow of a long day of intense heat is cast upon the land as darkness begins its reign of terror. The creatures of the day cower under the threat of new intruders making their way through the cold, brisk air that collide with anything that would dare cross their path.

The Night then gathers more strength and begins its rule. As the king of the blackness, it oversees all and becomes a terror for the day creatures. Nevertheless, just when all hope seems lost, a glimpse of light protrudes over the horizon and ends the uncertainty created by Night.

This passes unseen but shows that no matter what happens during the worst of times, the Sun will rise, and hope will come with it.

Matthew Harding

The gloaming dim of the eve invades all five senses. Hear the rustling of the leaves, breathe the bitterness of the air and smell the moisture and dewy grass.

The sound of crickets chirp wildly as the wind creates shadows. My eyes begin to play tricks on me. Looking toward the nighttime sky, the twinkling stars wink back at me.

Rebecca Wilkinson
Kathleen Willoughby

The air grows thick and cold; the gloaming is almost over. No one is in sight, for the cold and rapid winds have chased the people into their homes and animals to their dens, hoping to keep warm.

Yet, the brisk air manages to find its way through crevices and cracks. It slips through the floor planks and walls, spreading throughout the houses like a virus.

Peering out the window, one sees all amounts of debris being blown as if in a whirlwind. Night has finally come. I think I will add another log to the fire.

Vickie Donald

The night is like a warm blanket of darkness. Stars pattern the shadowy quilt as I doze beneath it. I sleep peacefully knowing I am safe.

The aroma rushes in, full of the smell of dozing flowers. The wind warms my face. Trees sway softly in the wind, their fragrance drifting far away. The clouds turn black and the night fills the air.

Autumn Blackwell

So lonely and quiet, so calm, so cool and dark. As Mother Nature changes its course, violent shades of shadows begin to awaken. The night becomes inkier, the crisp air thicker.

Beyond the sky of darkness are flocks of birds, glistening stars and far away galaxies. The night gives you peace and soothes the soul. Oh, the joy of the night. It is only here to admire—what a magnificent sense of tranquility.

Regine Pierre
Jacquis Taylor

The night sky was as black velvet, smooth and clear as the stars shone through the crisp air. A thick mist could be felt settling in the night. As the heat faded, the tempo of the day calmed into the cool evening. Day had passed.

As all light vanished, the darkening sky surrounded everything. Darkness engulfed me as the crickets sang their song. Day noises gradually softened into silence. Peace and tranquility overwhelmed me.

Settling into bed, the sounds of night animals were around me. Crickets slowly chirping, two owls searching for prey, a black cat as dark as the night moving—all making a part of the silent, peaceful night.

Jesse Keogh

Hey Mrs. Barger, Thanks for a great 8th grade year, love ya. Jesse Keogh

Night is darkness with the bright, glistening stars sparkling in the deep, black sky, and covering all like a blanket.

The breeze in the night air is neither warm nor cold, but sends chills down the back of the spine. The night's wind feels as if someone is brushing against one's arm.

You can hear the crickets chirp but little else in the darkness. Quietness. Oh, did I hear a pin drop?

Rachel Stanley

As the sky slowly dims, coldness increases. A wave of silence crashes against my ears. A whistling ceases the silence. With this comes a chilling wind and the fragrant smell of rain. But it is merely fog growing rapidly as I ponder. Vision begins to fade through the sudden darkness. Night has slowly crept upon us.

Billy Butler

As the sky dims, the shadows fall. Coolness increases as the humidity rises. Everything becomes silent. The night is slowly creeping upon us. The darkness overpowers the dim light of the moon, leaving the sky mysteriously black. Animals scamper for cover and rest. The air is as chilling as the wolf's howl. Slowly, stars pop up in the night. It is finally here.

Josh Lamie

The falling shadows cast a gloomy image upon the sidewalk. They flickered as the inn doors opened and closed. Shrinking, as the large man came closer, closer, closer. Stopping and staring at me, he seemed to be contemplating something. We stared at each other for what seemed to be hours. I felt sweat on my brow and chills running up my spine.

Then, as if nothing had happened, he slowly turned and drifted off into the night, never to be seen again…

Brennan Burke
John Smith

Now that day has come to an end,
The things of night will soon begin.
With the frogs croaking and the wind howling,
You can feel that night is surely there.
Now that you know that night is here, be very careful, be aware.

With the moon glaring and glowing down,
The animals can see its lonesome frown.
As coyotes howl to ease their pain,
A distant wind plows across the plain.

As the night comes to a certain end,
The nightly things will surely suspend.
But the night may now be gone away,
Remember, you only wait one more day.

Michael Carter

Night—the dark, desolate hours between the twilight and the gloaming. Creatures casually stride into the shadows. The world seen in the day no longer exists. The everyday life has vanished as has the brilliant, spectacular light projecting from the sun. Darkness engulfs the earth. There is a sound, suddenly nothing.

The mind constantly deceives its possesser. It sees a dimension of shadows never perceived. There is a fleeting sense of reality, nothing more.

Chasity Hogan
Don Sauls

You are a great principal Chasity ♥ u

The night air rolls in on the chill of a summer breeze. Crickets chirp and fireflies glow. Shadows of the midnight moon fall upon the lawn, the taste of salt as always on a summer night. Smelling the musky scent from the garden flowers relaxes and chases all your troubles away. Lying on the firm ground, staring at the stars, wondering whether to get up or close you eyes. Heavenly!

Chelsea Rodman
Megan Kirby

your a great principal! ♥ Chelsea Rodman

The falling shadows slip down across the dewy streets. Enough of seeing nothing but cars storming by and hearing the blare of horns and engines. The terrible stench of exhaust in the air always tasted. With the coming of the cozy, peaceful night, I am very comfortable.

Kyle Maas

As the night sets in, the silence runs deeper through my blood. The cries of sadness and despair are more apparent than ever, but they are drowned by the stillness of the dark. Even in the comfort of home, the darkness creeps deep into my soul.

Chance Jackson

The shadows were gazing at the lonely travelers. All were hiding in their beds, frightened that the shadows would fall upon their hopeless souls. This only happens once a midnight dreary.

There is a legend about the shadows. Of how they come and terrorize the helpless and misfortunate. Only when the great ball of flame is at rest at last are they safe.

But there is hope for the restless. Once the sun rises on the next dawn, the shadows will become one and they shall never return. Unless the shadows see a glimpse of darkness. Then, and only then, do the blackened shadows torment again.

Zach Benson
Zach Prichard

As the sun falls below the horizon, the nocturnal creatures come out to play. Owls call in the distance, and beams of light cast an eerie glow. All around are the sounds of creatures creeping. Brilliant silver wolves stream by upon the forest's carpet. Wild mushrooms fill the air with a tantalizing aroma. Shooting stars light the midnight sky as the smell of roses soars past the perfect blue waters with its crystalline surface. A perfume of lavender and lilac fills the air. Soon the sun will rise once again and shower the world with its own light.

David Klunk
Jordan Barnhardt

Falling shadows of night give a weary feeling to those below. A thousand candles of light scatter across the sky. The sounds of scattering animals and the thousand eyes of night bring frigid coldness as the dew settles. Impatience for the sun to rise and free me from this fear of the dark and all that the night touches plagues me. At last, the sun begins to ascend and my spirits rise. So, once again, I am free.

Kim Needleman

Darkness falls. Feel the night air upon your skin. Smell the fresh, cold scent of the night. The dew settles upon the ground. The air becomes thick and dreary. Hear the blowing of the trees and the falling of the leaves. The night is wondrous.

Wes Gray

The falling of night, screeching of wind, smell of moisture. Dark and dim. Black with light no more. Cool breeze comes through the window chilling the furniture, sense of fear, smell of musk.

Look of pure darkness. Sight of stars blind the weak. Shadows lurk no more.

Taste of cool air. As the moon glows, a feeling of security. Almost as if someone is watching over me. Eyes staring from the sky.

Mike Van Orden

The sky turns a bright orange. The beautiful sun is heading westward. The wind blows through the branches of the trees. The fresh scent of leaves falling as the temperature drops is a radiant sign that night has begun.

The moon rises as the sun falls, and the stars overlap the clouds. The owls awaken from their daily slumber.

Malcolm Lockridge

As the sun went down on the beach, the moon rose over the hill and you could feel the ocean breeze. Listening, you heard the waves crashing above the starry night as the sand crawled between your toes. While walking away from the dark, starry night, the smell of salt began to fade.

Slowly walking down the dark, narrow path, the only noise being made came from your feet quietly dragging along. The stars made the streetlights look dull and dim. The moon had become a crystal ball.

I watched lights turning off as I walked down the street. Taking the last step to the door, I turned and what I saw took my breath away.

Camille Ward

The night was as dark as the bottom of the ocean. The wind, swirling like a hurricane, sent a chill down my spine. Then the night became silent.

As I opened my mouth, the wind tasting of summer flowers spun on the tip of my tongue. Behind me, crickets chirped and a faint breeze swept through my hair.

Megan Coleman

As she lay watching the star called the Sun fall behind the horizon, she felt the darkness take over. The air blew by her, sending chills up her spine. She was afraid, terrified. An owl hooted and she was breathing heavily. She knew she had to get home. Running up the porch steps, she knew she had made it. As she flipped the light switch, she murmured, "The darkness is over for now."

Ryan Taylor

It is gloomy, and the night is about to arrive. The shadows fall. The smell is of wildflowers, and many sounds can be heard throughout the night. The wolves howling, frogs croaking, wind whistling, and crickets chirping. What a delight!

The night feels like a sensation when it is clear. To feel and smell the crisp air thicken. Knowing that night will soon end is disappointing, but then there is a brand new day coming.

Casey Novak

The air grows thick and cold. The crickets begin to chirp their peaceful songs. The animals begin to stir. The darkness rises, and the brightness falls.

The moon rises in the darkened sky. It is your only light. Night has come. The nocturnal wake from their daily rest and begin their hunt. This is nighttime.

Brooke Nichols

Night is a creature beyond its own power. People will not go out because the wind howls and the trees start to sway. When the sun creeps beyond the trees, the people leave because the night is on a neighborhood watch to kill. The night has no weakness.

Zach Appleton

As gloaming comes, the shadows fall. The night air starts to become moist and damp. The flowers close and the night smells arise. Everything that once was has now disappeared into the never-ending darkness. The air smells thick, moist and fresh. The dew starts to fall, and the fog engulfs me.

Josh Miller

Silence as night falls and darkness approaches. The streetlights come on, one by one. The clouds flow over us like a soft blanket. Darkness creeps over my shoulder as if I had been waiting for this moment.

Mychel Saddler

The night was coming. The winds blew bitter. The air tasted of honeysuckle and violets. The wind started to blow faster and faster. The air was crisp and the trees swayed to and fro. The moon rose out of the clouds, and then there was the beautiful night.

Amanda Billingsley

The night sky was like black velvet. It was smooth and clear as the stars shone through the crisp air. The night crept upon us like a lion stalking its prey. The crickets sang their songs and the fog was thick, making it hard to see. The dogs howled, and the owls hooted. The moon reflected off the lake, full and gleaming. As the fog lifted, the sky lightened, and the moon disappeared. Night was gone.

Justin Stubblefield

The night was dark and calm, with constellations lit with incredible brightness. Nocturnal animals awoke as others began their rest. The night is cool with a slight breeze which can send chills down your spine. How can the night be dark and bright at the same time?

Geoffrey Etheridge

Night is the time to wear black and the time to cover your head to hide from the dead. Night is the time for goblins to come out and for little ones to stay inside. Night is the time where evil plays and lurks for any and all. So, moms and dads, put your kids to bed, so they won't end up hurt instead. The night is Halloween.

Candice Moret

The night is like a warm blanket of darkness. Silence envelops me as the air thickens and turns cooler. I smile and drift peacefully off to sleep.

Stars pattern the shadowy quilt as I doze beneath it. I dream of my warmth and my contentment. I take a deep whiff of the placid atmosphere and sense things so wonderful that they are indescribable.

All of my melancholy feelings are pushed aside when I awake from my revelry and gaze at the constellations. I go back to sleep, knowing I am safe.

Mandy Strine

The cold air started to thicken as the sun drifted down through the trees and darkness crept into the sun's place. The wind began to whistle as it slithered through one's ear. The trees began to creak as they rocked back and forth through the wind's grip.

The rush of leaves on the ground began to dance around the trunks of the trees. In the sky the stars neither danced nor moved. The moon seemed to be at arm's length, but it kept moving between the stars.

Creatures began to explore through the darkness, tapping on trees and rustling in the leaves. A dim light began to peek through and the night was nearly gone.

The day was coming.

Ryan Gray

Seeing the flaming shooting stars, hearing the crickets call, tasting the sugar from a midnight snack, feeling the cool night air across your face and smelling the marshmallows from a nearby camp site are the signs of night.

Jeff Stinson

The night was cool as the breezes swept over me. It was a cloudless night, and the stars were bright. The fireflies soared in this breathtaking breeze. However, the night was very calm. As it got darker and darker, it was like inhaling the heavens themselves.

I listened to the hooting of the owls and the birds chirping gleefully. The cats meowed before settling down, and the dogs watched a while before closing their eyes.

The moon shone brightly through the clouds before I lay down, but it was soon covered by clouds. I closed my eyes and drifted away.

Heather Campbell

The night is as dark as the bottom of an endless pit.
As the moonlight hits my body the darkness and the
   wind conceals my soul.
Ghosts haunt me in my deepest thoughts as the thick air
Comes upon me and swirls around in my mind like a tornado.
As the ghosts in the wind whisper in my ear,
All there is to hear are cries of agony and pain of death.
For how I feel sorrow for these spirits that haunt me in the night.
But in this night there is no evil to fear, for in the end,
You are protected if you have faith.
For as long as you have a soul with faith, nothing can take that away.
In this darkest hour, in the moment of silence, you will be judged.
And as you call on Him to save you,
He will be there to guide you through this night.

Chris Knight

Thanks for getting me
out of tough times

Chris Knight

Menagerie

Time and again
Endings, beginnings.
A dark night, a pure dawn.
Do not fear what is coming
Or forget what has gone.

Jesse Hagan

"Freedom's Not Bought With Dust..."

What does that statement mean to you? What does freedom mean to you? Is it freedom of religion, freedom to live and go to school where you want? The truth is that all of those things are true. Freedom has many definitions, but one thing is always the same: it comes with a price. A high price.

Freedom is a wonderful thing. Most everyone will agree with that, but it cannot be "paid for" with something so worthless as dust. Most of the time it is paid for in human lives. These people, for the most part, have been members of the United States military and have given their lives to keep ours free.

When I say one must pay for freedom, I mean having freedom is similar to going to a store. Peoples' lives are the currency, and freedom is the gift.

Kristen Kellett

Family

Family is a thing you're born into,
    People you can depend on, through and through.
When you're feeling bad, they can make you feel better,
    With a hug, a phone call, or even a letter.
Someone to love, someone to love you.
    They'll always care, no matter what you do.
You're glad when they're born, you're sad when they die,
    But there's always someone to at least say, "Hi."
Family comes, and family goes,
    But we always have family, that everyone knows.

Stephen Brown

The Years Without Choices

I feel like a common peasant.
Wandering the halls through the crowds of people.
All of the faces silently staring.
Most of us hardly noticing.
Everyone not even caring.
The day is based on a system of rules and bells.
All of us like drones.
They try to herd us as if we were cattle.
Taking away our individuality.
Forcing us to obey, constantly we are punished.
Our sanity I feel is slowly seeping away
As we go through the years without choices.

Brian Hughett

Drifting

A cool, light breeze steals my mind,
Distracts me from my troubles.
I weep freely in sorrow and joy.
The feeling of warm salt streams down my face.

Surrounded by the clouds and grass,
I confess my day's events.
The wind whistles with understanding.
I now feel reborn.

Now I go to start a new day,
But I know that I'll be back
To tell the next day's problems,
Seeking the cool breeze.

Chris Neal

Those Days

I remember those days
    When nothing went wrong,
Besides the part we were missing
    Of that Disney movie song.
I remember those times
    When all we would do was play.
But to tell you the truth,
    That was back in the golden days.
I remember those moments.
    All we thought about was the newest dolls.
Now all we think about
    Is whether or not that hot guy will call.
I remember the school years
    When life was a spelling word.
But in the conversations today,
    The word "life" is often heard.
I remember the picture perfect times.
    We would dress all nice and neat.
I could only wish,
    Life was still that sweet.
I remember the heart-breaking day
    We found out the truth.
Life is really complicated,
    And there's really nothing we can do.
I still remember that morning,
    When we became friends.
That was soon to become
    The promising day that nothing could end.

Brandi Rolin

Eighth Grade

Eighth grade stinks,
It stinks so bad it reeks.
It stinks because the work is hard,
And the teachers are mean.
It's perfect!

Eighth grade is terrible
With all the pressure,
With all the things to do,
And still maintaining a life.
All the rushing is great!

Eighth grade stinks, and it's terrible.
I hope it never ends.

Elizabeth Cantrell

9/11

To the people who lost their lives.
To the husbands who lost their wives.

To the fathers who lost a son.
To the people who lost no one.

We all grieve in this time of pain
No matter what religion, location, or name.

How could someone do such a thing,
To take all these lives, just for fame?

My prayers go out to the people who are no more.
On this tragic day, hearts are scared and sore.

What could possess this one man
To make such an evil plan?

Ashes to ashes, dust to dust.
Now we have angels to watch over us.

Yet America is strong and will not give in.
However, we will never forget this terrible day of sin.

Dana Parsley

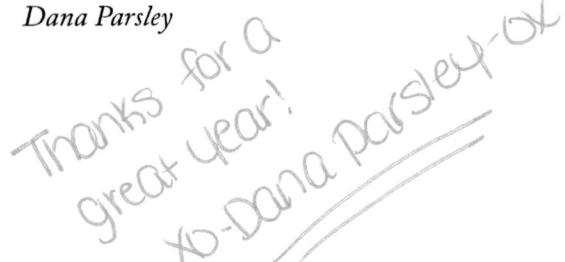

The Unknown Gadget

The head scientist came into the lab that morning holding a small box. "Good morning, everyone!" he said cheerfully.

"Good morning!" chorused the fellow scientists.

"We have something a little different to work on today. I hope nobody objects to a bit of change."

Of course, nobody did, so the scientist proceeded with his plans. He held up the box.

"There is a gadget of some sort in this box. I don't know what it is, but there are clues on this sheet of paper that came with it."

"What are the clues?" asked one scientist.

The head scientist began to read the words on the paper. "I am constantly changing. I am unpredictable. With me, sometimes really great things happen, but sometimes really awful things can happen. Does anyone know yet?"

Nobody knew.

So he continued reading, "One day you will look back on me and laugh. Some people take advantage of me. Some don't. They waste me as if they could always go back and get another one of me. They can't. Once I am gone, I am gone. There is no turning back."

That was all the paper said, and the scientists were left stumped.

"Let's open the box," said another scientist.

They all agreed.

The only thing in the box was a tiny piece of paper that said, "Life."

Lindsey Dye

Fate

The present is changing
And the past is taking on new perspectives.
The future, however, still lies open.
We try to speculate
What it holds for us,
But we will never know
Until the future becomes the present.
So the truth is, we can guess
And predict all we want in vain,
Because what the future becomes
…is up to fate.

Tasha Bronner

Time and Again

Time and again
Endings, beginnings.
A dark night, a pure dawn.
Do not fear what is coming
Or forget what has gone.

Time and again
Hellos, good-byes.
In your heart, not your sight.
The friends you've made are in your soul...
Brighten your heart and make you whole.

Time and again
Reassurance, survival.
Things work out as they should.
So, my dear, please dry your eyes.
There is no such thing as forever good-byes.

Jesse Hagan

A Day in the Life of Me

My school day starts
As I hop on the bus,
And it's hardly ever
Without a fuss.
A few minutes pass;
Our bus comes to a stop,
Another half hour
And I'm at my desktop.

I start the day off with
A moment of silence,
The Pledge of Allegiance
And character to prevent violence.
We sing the National Anthem,
Opening with "O, say can you see"
And closing with "the land of the free."

Class has now begun.
The bell has rung.
As the teacher gives us work,
Everyone's face forms
A disgusted smirk.
Girls roll their eyes,
Guys groan.
Then the teacher
Forms a forceful tone.
Some get detention,
And, if necessary, in-school suspension!

I wait at the edge of my seat
Then jump to my feet.
As I hear the bell to leave,
I rush to the bus,
Roll down the window,
And enjoy the breeze.

Finally I'm home
Wanting loads of food.
But my mom says,
"Not till after dinner,"
Which puts me in a grouchy mood.

After I eat, and my
Homework is complete,
I can watch some TV,
Then fall asleep.

Lacey Greene

You're a great principal! ♡ -Lacey

We Don't Notice

Changes happen to us in our lives,
    But we don't notice.

Those changes can be good or drastic,
    But we don't notice.

Changes can usually be very hard on us,
    We do notice that.

Whether we do or don't notice changes,
    They happen to us anyway.

Ben Steger

I Pray For My Country

I pray for my country
And the people who lost their lives,
The evil ones who terrorized us
And the victims who survived.

I pray for my country,
The security we have lost,
For the policemen and firefighters
And for what their bravery cost.

I pray for the families
Of the people not yet found
From the morning the World Trade Towers
Were hit and then fell to the ground.

I pray for world peace,
The kind that escapes our hearts today.
But with wisdom and guidance
I have faith in the U.S.A.

Courtney Tucker

Desire Not Attire

It's not the Nikes on your feet
That drop your spirit
When you get beat
It's not the number on your back
That steals the ball
Or stops the attack
It's not the headband, jersey, or socks
That step up to the line
And shoot the rock
It's your heart and your will
That take over your game
Because without them you're like the others,
The same
There is nothing on you or in your attire
That comes through in the fourth quarter
Like your desire

Casey Pigue

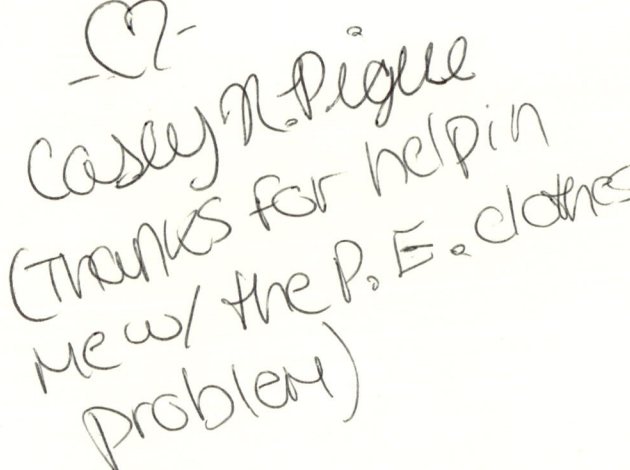

9/11

9/11
These numbers mean a lot
They mean agony and pain
On this day bombings happened
And buildings fell down

One thing that didn't fall
Was our freedom and justice
This day meant a lot to everyone
And no one will be able to take that
Moment away

When people stand up and fight
For our freedom

Jessica Manshadi

I Wonder

Once, on a snowy evening, I was sitting on my porch watching the other kids play. I had my coat and gloves on, ready to go and play, too, but I couldn't. I can't even stand on my own two mangled feet. I've spent my whole life in a wheelchair. I can't even remember one day that I stood up. I can't go anywhere. I wish I could run and play with the other kids.

While I was sitting there I thought about how much fun it would be to run, jump, and swim with my so-called friends. How wonderful it would be to be released from all this pain. My tears were forming into icicles. I wonder if...I will ever be free.

Justin Hastings

Lemons

Lemons are scented
Fresh as the morning breeze
Tasteful lemons—
    More sour than candy

Yellow lemons—
    Not brighter than the sun
Nor the stars when they are shining
At their fullest

Dee Gregory

Lean On Me

You came to me and I had never heard you speak.
You simply fell into my arms and asked me not to go.
I never knew it meant that much to you,
Until I saw a strange twitch in your eye.
You had told me before, you could never cry.
But I knew you were about to break your promise.
I did not understand why you waited so long.
It was almost too late, then I thought you were
      the only one to stop me.
Finally, you had done what I was hoping you would do.
Soon, I had to tell another that I could not do what he wished
Because I had found that I could not spend the rest of my life
With one who could not lean on me.

Jessica Powell

Hello
     Mrs. Barger,
Thany for all your
Help this year.
     -♡-
          Jessica

Printed in the United States
4111